CONTENTS

On The Same Theme

by Indy Jean Arden

Theme: We must care and be knowledgeable to ensure our existence in a seemingly indifferent universe.

On The Same Theme

by Indy Jean Arden

And Cain talked with Abel his brother: and it came to pass, when they were in the field, that Cain rose up against Abel his brother, and slew him.

And the Lord said unto Cain, Where is Abel thy brother? And he said, I know not: Am I my brother's keeper?

And he said, What hast thou done? the voice of thy brother's blood crieth unto me from the ground.

And now art thou cursed from the earth, which hath opened her mouth to receive thy brother's blood from thy hand;

When thou tillest the ground, it shall not henceforth yield unto thee her strength; a fugitive and a vagabond shalt thou be in the earth…

Genesis Chapter 4, Verses 8 through 12
King James Version

On The Same Theme

by Indy Jean Arden

And behold, a certain lawyer stood up, and tempted him, saying, Master, what shall I do to inherit eternal life?

He said unto him, what is written in law? How readest thou?

And he answering said, Thou shalt love the Lord thy God with all thy heart, and with all thy soul, and with all thy strength, and with all thy mind; and thy neighbour as thyself.

And he said unto him, Thou has answered right: this do, and thou shalt live.

But he willing to justify himself, said unto Jesus, And who is my neighbour?

And Jesus answering said, A certain man went down from Jerusalem to Jericho, and fell among thieves, which stripped him of his raiment, and wounded him, and departed, leaving him half dead.

And by chance there came down a certain priest that way: and when he saw him, he passed by on the other side.

And likewise a Levite, when he saw him, and passed by on the other side.

But a certain Samaritan, as he journeyed, came where he was: and when he saw him, he had compassion on him,

And went to him, and bound up his wounds, pouring in oil and wine, and set him on his own beast, and brought him to an inn, and took care of him.

And on the morrow when he departed, he took out two pence, and gave them to the host, and said unto him, Take care of him; and whatsoever thou spendest more, when I come again, I will repay thee…

Luke Chapter 10, Verses 25 through 35 King James Version

On The Same Theme

Cynical Quotations and Carmelita Jokes

by Indy Jean Arden

1. "Nigger" was the point of slavery.

2. God has always been indifferent to the poor - kinda like humans.

Carmelita says: Don't be absent and missing, don't be absent and missing like pussy in Elton John's house.

3. When everything is going right you are being set up.

4. Fight no one for an inheritance - just split with the hitman.

Carmelita says: Don't be absent and missing like a Mormon wife with a young husband.

5. When you creep at night be sure to use the right glass cutter on the right window - Just saying - not that that ever happened to me - recently.

Carmelita says: Don't be absent and missing like a French woman with a daily bath.

Carmelita has a knock knock joke:
Knock knock
Who is there?
July
July who?
July like Trump.

6. When lies comfort, we find religion.

7. Happy is the man whose girlfriend is meticulous about his wife's schedule.

8. Knowledge is always reeling from the blows of ignorance.

9. Joy in your soul is just the Jamaican Primo…or is it from Colorado?

10. Faith is necessary to set up the deception for the control.

> Carmelita says: Don't be absent and missing like a Jamaican who doesn't know where to find good weed.

11. If you do not know truth when you hear it, yep, you are a politician or even worse a scientologist or even worse Florida man.

12. Took some Viagra then some younger guy took my girl. Yep, life is hard and one other thing too.

Carmelita says: Don't be absent and missing like a tight booty in prison.

13. Arguing means no one is listening.

14. Seek balance, knowledge will follow, for it is knowledge that tells you to seek balance.

15. The poor should never be afraid of knowledge.

Carmelita says: Don't be absent and missing like a priest with short fingers.

16. It can be argued that everyone has the right to be ignorant, but why would anyone want that right?

Carmelita has a knock knock joke:
Knock knock
Who is there?
Santa
Santa who?
Santa to the bus station; hope the bitch never comes back!

17. If you don't believe in science, why go to hospitals?

18. It is not that atheists are wrong; it is that all the gods are well-hidden.

Carmelita says: Don't be absent and missing like the bullied who is not planning revenge.

19. Lies can be comforting, but it is truth that is practical.

20. Beware the charming; they are setting up the exploitation.

21. Name a god who is not parochial in origin and you will probably have the right one.

Carmelita says: Don't be absent and missing like a strap-on that hates being moist.

22. They say that a dog is man's best friend. I say, what about people who know you have money?

Carmelita says: Don't be absent and missing like a Trump truth.

Carmelita says: Don't be absent and missing like fair and balanced on Fox News.

Carmelita says: Don't be absent and missing like Biden's clarity.

Carmelita says: Don't be absent and missing like education in the ghetto.

23. Justice is balanced on the backs of the poor.

24. Some Christians act as if suppression is their birthright.

25. There are only two kinds of people in this world: the thoughtful and the thoughtless; perhaps there is a third kind but they are too busy hiding from the thoughtless.

26. 98% of all morality is property.

27. The Ultimate Wisdom: Do unto others…

On The Same Theme

Two Pebbles in a Flood - A Fable of Our Time

by Indy Jean Arden

-23-

"I am not going to make a political argument against your plans Jill. I am going to make an emotional one. For some years now, I have been thinking of humans as pebbles in a flood, helpless in an uncaring universe. I do not want to believe that. I want to believe in God."

"I have heard it said that you are an atheist - you can't believe in God."

"Yes, I can; Just not the god of this culture. I want to believe in a universal God."

"I have heard it said that the God of the Bible is the universal God."

"I do not think so. He sent a flood."

"So?"

"Some of those who drowned in the flood were babies, little crawling children, children learning how to walk, innocent children, pebbles in a flood; babies in the womb. That God committed abortion."

Jill's eyes widened in surprise, in realization. She had never thought of that, had never realized that. "What do you want me to do?"

"Have the baby and give it to me."

"You would want 'my' baby?"

"Yes, to save your baby from being just a pebble, I would take your child. Your child shall be my child. The God of the Hebrews could have saved those babies with a snap of his fingers. He chose not to. You can make a better choice. I will gladly have your baby."

"You are only seventeen, you are going to college."

"Yes, but I will have help. My family, my mother, my father, my grandparents. We are a liberal family who believes that indifference to the pain and suffering of humans does not ultimately make any sense."

"Are you telling me that my child will make a difference to humanity? I have heard that argument before and then I look on the internet and I see children suffering all over the world."

"I am not telling you that your child will make a difference. Your child could be another Hitler. The thing though about evil is that it cannot thrive without stupid political support. You were stupid when you had unprotected sex with Jack. I was stupid when I got carried away with Jessie. What I am telling you is that I am a better woman than you are. I would preserve life. You would destroy it. I want your child."

"My child? My child? I…I…I just don't want anything of Jack to be inside of me. I hate him. It has been horrible. You do not know. You are too goody-two-shoes to know."

"Tell me."

"So many teens, especially girls, make fun of me. They think I'm stupid and easy. I am not easy. I am not a slut. You know what they say about me?"

"No."

"They made up a poem:

Jack and Jill went up the hill
To get some wet water
Jack strut down; Jack pimped down
And Jill received only laughter.

"It hurts, you have no idea how it hurts. I used to have a life."

"You still do. I swear."

"How can you be so sure?"

"I am sure because I read. Pregnancy is not the end of the world. Women get pregnant all the time. I am going to call June. She will connect me with the right people… The right people… I just realized how I'm going to help Janice."

"How?"

"I'm afraid I cannot tell you. You have other concerns. Your health, your baby's health and your education."

On The Same Theme

A Marriage in Beckford

by Indy Jean Arden

-13-

The cheering was never going to end. At least not for a while. Then Fenton Fullmer stepped forward, stood beside "Tildy, Tildy, Tildy" ...and held up the ring. Instantly the cheering stopped. It was as if all the cheering sounds of the world fled into hiding, into that secret place where sounds go when silence is in command.

The little blue box, containing the ring, nestled securely in Fenton's uplifted palm. Slowly Fenton lowered the box to his side.

"Beckfordians," There was a hint of hopelessness in his voice, "you need not worry yourself with a vote." He did not continue.

He saw the confusion in his people's eyes.

He was starting to enjoy this. He cautioned himself not to become too cocky. He is The Guardian of the Ring; He did not want to be seduced by the power of any office or position, unlike Tildy.

He spoke now with a certain confidence and swagger in his voice.

"There is a different way in which Beckfordians settle disputes. We do so by way of a Challenge of Wisdom."

Fenton saw the instant interest in his people's eyes. To invoke a Challenge of Wisdom meant that the person being challenged must accept the challenge or be instantly defeated and anything - anything - that the challenger asked for, providing that it is not illegal or immoral, must be granted. It was the Beckfordian way. Much like in a Formal Speech Contest the loser had no choice but to accept defeat graciously.

Fenton knew that he had to set the conditions for the challenge.

"I, Fenton Fullmer, Guardian of the Ring, I challenge Matilda Wainwright, Liaison of Beckford, to a Challenge of Wisdom. If I should win, I have but four requests to ask of my people.

"One, the term mule or mulish in reference to barren women shall evermore be a taboo in Beckford."

Fenton did not pause to assess his people's reaction. Their reaction at this point really did not matter.

"Two, barren women will not be encouraged to migrate to foreign simply because of their state."

"Three, barren women shall be allowed to attend any and all marriages if they so choose."

There was a gasp at this from the gathered crowd. Fenton ignored it.

"Four, and this is the most important. Barren women henceforth shall be allowed to marry Beckfordian men!"

The outraged looks that Fenton received would have sliced him into many pieces if such a thing was possible in this world. But such a thing is not possible by the laws of physics. And by the laws of the Challenge of Wisdom every assembled Beckfordian had to remain steadfastly quiet until the challenge was complete. Fenton was grateful for that rule.

He bowed to Matilda. "Out of respect for your age and position, the Liaison may speak first."

Matilda recognised Fenton's trick. Though she was absolutely sure that she would win, it was not good strategy to speak first. In speaking first, one reveals some of one's strategy. A sharp opponent then had a few moments to revive and improve her own strategy.

Thinking quickly, and pretending to a graciousness she did not feel, Tildy bowed in return. "There is no one here," she calmly announced, "whose ceremonial power is more respected than the Guardian of the Ring, that being true, out of respect to your position, it is only fair and considerate that I, even the Office of Liaison, yield to you. If, however you lose this Challenge of Wisdom, things shall remain as they have always been."

There was a quick look of disappointment in Fenton's eyes. He saw the smiles of Beckford, sensing that surely, he would be defeated.

Fenton gave a quick severe nod to the Liaison, accepting her terms. Now it was time to cut her deeply with the one and single bit of wisdom that would win for him, and his love, and her kind, the day.

"Beckfordians," He announced with a confidence born of certainty, "I have but one bit of wisdom to impart to you.

"This bit of wisdom concerns a certain prediction made by the Esau." All of Beckford turned their eyes to look at the Esau. He did not want to meet their eyes. They turned their eyes back to the Guardian of the Ring.

"It was not so long ago," said Fenton, "that Dorothy Simpson, soon to be Dorothy Sinclair, became what is now being called the 'Beckfordian Legend.'" Dorothy bowed to the now curious audience.

"But," said Fenton, "what of the loser of that particular contest, the loser, Paulette Falconer?" Paulette standing steadfast beside her former rival bowed to Beckford. "There is a prediction concerning her that most of you do not know." Fenton paused for a few moments.

"After the contest, the Esau went to console her, as is customary in such cases. And while consoling her the Esau said: 'Paulette, indeed you shall be as a mother to Beckford, children - even children of foreign - shall come and bow down to you."

Fenton could see that his audience did not get what he was driving at. They had no clue. Time to enlighten them.

"Please," he said, "let me see by the raising of your hands, how many of you doubt the Esau's words."

Fenton waited. Not a single hand was raised.

"Yes!" he shouted, "It is as I thought it would be. Every single one of us knows that the Esau's predictions are always true. He is the genetic griot. He approves all marriages to ensure that Beckford has healthy and beneficial children.

"And-he-has-said that children of foreign-FOR-EN-ERS shall come to Beckford and bow down to one of our very own. FOR-EN-ERS shall pay the greatest respect to one of Beckfordian loins.

"But…" Fenton held the 'but' and allowed the anticipation to tantalize his people. He held the 'but' to the very edge of impertinence then he said: "What shall they find when they get here?

"They shall find a proud and defiant people, well educated, and accomplished.

"They shall also find a people that allowed their children to grow up in prejudice against some of their very own kind." Fenton rushed on, determined to drive home his point. "They shall marvel that such a proud and defiant, well educated people, would allow such prejudice." Now Fenton shouted at the top of his voice. "And they shall pity our precious Beckfordian children! There is no prejudice in foreign against barren women! They shall pity our children!"

Fenton allowed his speech to sink in. He let it sink in deeply. He saw their eyes. The staggering shame was an actual physical force. Fenton actually staggered back. He gathered himself. He had already won, he knew. But there was one more thing he had to say.

He did not shout this time but none-the-less his voice boomed.

"Let me see the hands of each and every Beckfordian who can accept the idea - the very reality - of FOR-EN-ERS pitying our precious jewels; our children." Fenton waited. No hand rose. He knew there would not be any. The day was his, more importantly, the day was his woman and her kind. With a sweeping mock bow, he said to the Liaison, "Now it is your turn to speak."

Matilda knew, all of Beckford knew, there was no way under the stars that any Beckfordian could argue that foreigners should pity the precious jewels of Beckfordian union: their children.

But she was not the Liaison of Beckford for nothing. She could not win this day. Beckfordian psychology prevented any avenue to victory.

Matilda bowed to Fenton, why not? Truly his victory was remarkable. She raised her staff and all eyes rested on her.

"My fellow Beckfordians," she calmly spoke, not a hint of pride in her voice, "I must confess that I did not see the coming of this day. I am the Liaison of Beckford and I should have seen it coming. I feel that I have failed you. You who have given me your full support and your trust. Because of me, in the coming years, there could have been a scandalous tragedy in Beckford.

"It is clear to me now that there must be changes in Beckford. It will take time for the full implementation of barren women receiving their full

Beckfordian rights. If Beckford so desires I will remove myself as Liaison. Perhaps someone more fit should lead this 'full implementation.'"

It did not take long, as Tildy knew it would not.

It started slowly but in less than a few seconds her nickname resounded throughout the whole of Upper Yard: "Tildy! Tildy! Tildy!...!" The people would not stop shouting. With the screaming of her name (Matilda rather liked her nickname now), the people were saying, we were wrong too, there is no one more qualified to lead this 'full implementation' than you, "Tildy! Tildy! Tildy! Tildy!..."

-14-

The Mystic Side

by Indy Jean Arden

Far from the maddening crowds
It should never be forgotten,
That buffaloes don't fly anymore.
Can the flowers sparkle brightly,
When clouds lock in the sun?

And if I should leave you lady,
Would your tears wash away the stones?
Jehovah has blessed me well with wisdom.
I-don't-worship-idly.
I keep counsel in my heart.
Go! Keep counsel in your church.

Distraction, distraction and inner peace is lost,
For Jones has a new car,
And your wagon has been dented by the Winding Road,
But the devil got tired of your blames,
And left you to your own schemes,
Some are losing houses, money and land,
It gets cold on city streets,
No buffaloes hide to keep warm.

The circle has been closed a long time lady,
The birds of messages now are gone,
And buffaloes don't fly anymore,
Someone said now they only run.

The Elders left us long ago,
(Perhaps pressing business in the cosmos,)

They were on the Mystic Side of course,
…And did us no favors,
Yet still we know,
Can the flowers sparkle brightly,
When clouds lock in the sun?

-The most famous piece of literature in Beckford.
Author Unknown.
Credited to the First and Greatest Esau.

The Racist Tree

by Indy Jean Arden

Just fell out of the barren racist tree
Deceitful Donald says he has a job for me
Kicking little Mexican children into the sea
A better metaphor there could never be
I love you Donald, I swallow your pee
Thank you Massa, for guarding the racist tree

I love it when you talk so mean
'Cause we get it, that's the scene
Codes and lies that's what we want
Don't want to hear shit that we can't
Give us mythology in your posted views
Conway says, facts are lies, fuck the news

Just fell out of the barren racist tree
We celebrate the lies, the lies, one, two, three…
We love you Donald, lies will set us free
A better metaphor there could never be
Kicking little Mexican children into the sea
We love you Massa, we swallow your pee

Some people say you got that SPC -
Small Peter Complex - Well, that's for me
So I beat my woman and I ignore school
Don't give a damn if you think I'm a fool
Trump's my man, he got that SPC -
Small Peter Complex - Well, that's for me.

Just fell out of the barren racist tree
Yes, I'm mean and ignant as could be
Not my fault - I got that SPC
Deceitful Donald says he got that job for me
Kicking little Mexican children into the sea
Hope it's not a lie that he gives away for free
'Cause… I just fell out of the barren racist tree…

<u>The Last Time I Saw Mich-el</u>

by Indy Jean Arden

"Shhh, listen my child,
Gentle daughter meek, so mild,
'Tis time now that you know,
The truth of things before you grow,
For some will tell you tales untrue,
For spite to see what you will do.
So listen my child,
Gentle daughter meek, so mild,
I was a woman of full independence,
Oh, how I revel in my brilliance,
And all the men did stare at me,
Oh child, a grand show for all to see.
The other women sowed venom spitefully,
I cared less, I was dark, I was lovely.
Now hush my child,
Gentle daughter meek, so mild,
Mich-el said that beauty is no disgrace,
But then how do you see beyond your face?
Mich-el is a poet and well he rhymed,
I felt chastised and duly fined.
I tried, I schemed, so hard to win his love,
Oh, but it is hard for hawk to change to dove.
Be still my child,
Gentle daughter meek, so mild,
Only once did my charms win his passion,
Oh, how wonderful now my motherly mission.
The last time I saw Mich-el
-Something was different, I could tell -
It was on Christmas day
And this is what he had to say:

'I've heard through the vine, you've converted,'
And I said, 'yes, yes, my life is now amended.'
He smiled, and soon we will be together,
A family, you, me, and your father.
And you are so much like him my child,
Gentle daughter meek, so mild."

- written as a gift to the seven-year-old daughter of Juanita Major, supermodel, and the Beckfordian's greatest assassin - The Beckfordian Black Widow - From "The Children of the Storm"
by Indy Jean Arden

The Day No Child Would Go To School

by Indy Jean Arden

-1-

David Stoner knew that he could save Fifer. But to save him, he was going to need some help; he was going to need lots of help, because no one was going to listen to a nine-year-old child, a mere pickny. But that was okay for David had a plan. The plan was perfect and it could not fail.

David leaned his slender dark-brown body against the tall coconut tree that was on the edge of the school yard of Liberty Grammar School. He reviewed some of what he knew.

It had been over two weeks now, a whole fourteen days since Fifer had been arrested for murder and thrown into jail without bail. David did not know exactly what bail was, but he knew enough to know that without "bail" one could not get out of jail. Fifer was going to be tried for murder. Murder! And according to all of the adults, Fifer would be found guilty and would be sent to prison. Prison! That was a most certain outcome, according to all of the adults. The only question was whether Fifer was going to spend life in prison or be put to death by lethal injection. David did not like the word lethal. He also did not like the word injection.

David knew that he still had a lot more thinking to do. Fifer's real name is Mr. Peter Grant. But no child ever calls him that. To every single child in Beckford and the surrounding towns, he is "Fifer," because he made bamboo flutes, or fifes, for the children. The children in Beckford called him the Beckfordian Santa Claus. Beckfordians did not celebrate Christmas; without Christmas there could not be a Santa. But there was a Fifer.

Almost, as if by magic, Fifer would appear with a fife just when a child seemed to need one.

And now, they are saying that this magical man had committed murder. David knew it was not true. All Beckfordian children knew it was not true. The radio, the television, the newspapers, and the adults were saying that Fifer had murdered “that man,” Ronald Lintsram, because Fifer did not like what Mr. Lintsram was saying on the radio. David knew that many adults did not like what Mr. Lintsram was saying about “politics,” but Fifer was not one of those adults. Fifer did not care about no Mr. Lintsram. Fifer only cared about two things, delivering mail in the town of Chapelville and making flutes for children.

But the adults were saying that Fifer had lured Mr. Lintsram down by the bamboo grove and had killed him with a blow to the back of Mr. Lintsram’s head. The adults said that Fifer was the only one there, so it must have been him. But David and all Beckfordian children knew that Fifer only went to the bamboo grove when he was going to cut the young bamboos to make fifes. So if he went deep into the grove, someone else could have come along and hit Mr. Lintsram over the head to kill him. It was amazing to David that adults could not see the obvious.

David had spoken to his father about all the things he had heard. “Dad, I know Fifer is innocent. He did not kill ‘that man,’ I know.”

His dad had hesitated before answering. They were walking home on the winding tree-covered path that served as the school road. David liked for his dad to come and walk home with him. He was a big responsible boy now and it was best to walk and talk with a grown man instead of your mother. Mom never seemed to understand that he was a big responsible boy now. Dad always understood.

Dad sighed, “all the wise elders of Beckford know that Fifer is innocent. His innocence will not save him.”

David froze. He was still walking right alongside his dad, keeping up with his father’s longer strides, but none-the-less, he froze. Inside, he felt his heart stop beating.

When his heart finally resumed beating, he stopped walking, “no, dad, no."

Dad reversed his direction, came to his son and bent down. “Would you like a shoulder ride?”

“No, dad, no.”

Dad reached out and held his hand, and somehow David's little nine-year-old legs found the strength, the knowledge, the power, to resume walking.

"Dad, we are 'Beckfordians,' can we not help Fifer?"

Dad hesitated and somehow David knew the answer before his father spoke.

"Son, this is a matter of Law, Jamaican Law. And while we 'Beckfordians' are loyal citizens of Jamaica, Beckfordians do not interfere with Jamaican Laws. To do so would put us at risk. Our first and foremost responsibility is to protect ourselves. We protect ourselves by not bringing undue attention to Beckford. We will not risk ourselves to protect a Chapelviller."

-2-

Chapelviller, Chapelviller, Chapelviller… The word kept rolling around in little David Stoner's head as if it was the only thought his brain was capable of holding. He shook his head. He had to think. Though he did not want to think about Chapelvillers, he had to think.

Chapelvillers did not like Beckfordians. Beckfordians did not like Chapelvillers. David was not sure why. Chapelvillers are Christians. Beckfordians are, are…well, Beckfordians are…just Beckfordians. Though the two towns are neighbors, they really had very little to do with each other. Except Fifer was different. So different that no Beckfordian child ever thought of him as a Chapelviller. And now, he was in jail for a crime he did not commit.

But little David had a plan. He straightened up, moving away from the coconut tree, to put the first part of his plan into action.

Her name was Marcia Maycon and she was the prettiest (at least David thought so) and the most popular girl in the whole fourth grade. She was so popular not because she was pretty but because she was the fastest girl, under twelve years old, in all of Liberty Grammar School. She was faster even than most boys. She was faster than David. David was proud of her. He was mostly proud of the fact that he was her pickny friend. A pickny friend is someone under the age of twelve who “liked” someone of the opposite sex. You became a boyfriend or girlfriend at the age of twelve.

A lot of good things happened at the age of twelve, thought David. Boys got to wear long pants and girls got to wear “mature bras,” unless they matured early and just had to wear them before twelve.

He was only nine, still in short pants, a khaki shirt and khaki short pants, the school uniform, the school symbol of boyhood. Girls always wore their blue skirts and white blouses at school, their uniforms did not change at twelve years old. But girls were girls, they were smart and pretty and for the most part they only played girl games. But one girl was as good at boy games as any boy. That girl - Marcia Maycon - was a key part of David’s plan.

-3-

Marcia rested against one of the many dwarf orange trees that surrounded the playground. She had just finished chasing down boys all over the school yard. She had caught them too, everyone. She needed to catch her breath before the school bell sounded, starting school for the day.

David gave her a few moments to catch her breath.

She had seen him coming towards her and she smiled, exhaustingly, encouragingly at him.

He did not wish her a good morning.

“You are going to help me,” he said.

She frowned at him.

He realized his breach of good manners.

“I’m sorry,” he said. “Good morning.”

"Good morning," she sweetly said, glad that it did not take him long to realize his impolite behavior. David was bright. That was the main reason she liked him. He was handsome too, a dark handsomeness that made them a good looking pickny pair with her own almost as dark prettiness. She knew she was pretty because all the boys told her so.

"You seem eager to talk to me," said Marcia. "I saw you watching me when I was playing chase." She giggled. "I like when you watch me."

David was silent, a little embarrassed. He did not know what to say. He did not want to be impolite again.

"It's okay. It's okay, David, you are my pickny friend. Everyone knows that."

David smiled, feeling more confident. "I was watching you because I need your help with something 'very important.'" David wondered if he had stressed the "very important' enough. Obviously, he had.

Marcia's face was a mixture of curiosity and eagerness. "I'll help you if I can David." The soft look in her eyes seemed to say, "surely you know that."

David took a while to respond. He did not know how to say it, so he just said it. "We are going to save Fifer," he said. There, it was out, now he would have to be really careful how he explained it to her.

A frown lingered on Marcia's face. She finally spoke, "Two picknys cannot save Fifer. No one can save him. Chapelville, those Christians, cannot save him, and Beckford will not help to save a Christian, even if we could."

David only smiled boldly at her. He hoped he was acting the part of boldness just right.

Obviously, he was.

Marcia's face became one of total curiosity.

"What?" she said, "what?" But her tone said, "David I know you, you are up to some delicious mischief. Don't you dare get involved in some delicious mischief without including me." Her reaction was exactly as David had hoped. He did not hesitate.

"We can save Fifer. We the children, the fourth graders of Beckford, but if my plan does not work our behavior may attach scandal to our names."

"Scandal?" Marcia said the word slowly. There was a hint of fear in her voice.

All Beckfordians are afraid of scandal. A good name, a fine reputation is Beckfordian gold. All Beckfordians guarded such a golden coin jealousy. In her nine-year-old heart Marcia was polishing her golden coin. She did not want to lose it.

"But," said David, "a risk of scandal, a tiny risk, is worth it to save the life of Fifer, who has brought all Beckfordian picknys so much happiness."

Marcia knew that David was right. Scandal was terrible, but David had a plan, if the plan worked then there would be no scandal. If the plan failed then there would be shame, scandal attached to her name, but there would also be pride, pride in knowing that she had tried her best to help Fifer, a giver of happiness. Even scandal, it seemed to her, was worth the risk.

"How can we help Fifer?" she asked.

David smiled. Almost a mature smile. Marcia had never liked it when picknys acted like adults.

"We can help him by using psychology," said David.

"We are picknys," responded Marcia, "we do not know any psychology. Psychology is for grown people."

"No," said David, "I will show you how it works…What are the two most important things in Beckford Town?"

Marcia did not answer.

David restated the question. "What do adults say are the two most important things in Beckfordian culture?"

Marcia knew what adults said. She answered with no enthusiasm. "They say that child rearing and education are the two most important things in Beckfordian culture."

"Yes, you have it right." David gave her a big encouraging smile. She seemed not to notice. He trudged on, "we are picknys, we can do nothing about child rearing, but, we are picknys, we are involved in education." He stopped, letting Marcia take it all in. He resumed, "what if all the fourth graders decided that we will not go to school until Fifer is free? What would the adults do?"

Marcia wanted to think quickly but she found that she could not. This was such a large question. Too large. She had to take it in portions, like fractions. She was good at fractions. Every Beckfordian child loved learning. But also, every Beckfordian child loved Fifer. Which was the greater love? She did not know. She felt foolish. She looked into her pickny friend's eyes for help.

"We will only be out of school for a day, at the most," said David, "but the adults will not know that. They will think we will be out for a long time and education being so important, they will do what they can to free Fifer. I am sure of it."

Marcia was not sure. She was not sure simply because she could not think about something so large. It really wasn't much like fractions at all. Psychology was much harder than fractions. But one thing she was absolutely sure of, her pickny friend, David, knew a lot more about psychology than she did. She was going to help him. She did not like the fact that she was in fact jealous that David knew so much more about a subject that was not taught in grammar school.

-4-

Marcia was much more efficient in her help than David had anticipated. Marcia went directly to the second most popular girl in the fourth grade, Dora Conver. She was a pretty brown girl with Indian-like features, long curly hair, and a big bright smile. She was not popular for all those things. She was popular because she "knew" all about the Beckfordian Legend, Mrs. Dorothy Sinclair.

Dora was famous for telling every fourth grader that her name was derived from Dorothy and that when she grew up she was going to win a Formal Speech Contest just like her idol Mrs. Sinclair had won, and that she was going to live happily ever after with the man she would win. Dora had a flare for dramatic speech; everyone listened to Dora. So it was not surprising when Dora, like a mother hen, collecting up her wayward chicks, gathered all the fourth graders in the middle of the school yard. It was now time for David.

David felt proud. He felt tall. He knew this must be how it feels to be an adult. He would speak to them as if he was in fact an adult. He must not lose them now. Soon enough there will come a challenge to stop him. But he had thought long and hard about that and he had the answer; he hoped. His father had taught him that there are many challenges in this world but no challenge was so great that it could not be overcome by the proper use of psychology.

David knew that his father would not have lied to him. "Fourth graders," he boldly said, "all the adults say that Fifer cannot be saved. We are Beckfordians. All Beckfordians know that there is understanding in Beckford. I know that the understanding, the wisdom, of our adults can be used to save Fifer, but they will not use it to save him. They say it is because Beckfordians do not get involved with Jamaican Laws. But that is not the reason." He paused, letting the anticipation build in his classmates. "That is not the reason and I can prove it…What if a Beckfordian was falsely accused of murder? Would not all of Beckford move to free him or her? But we lift not a finger, not one single finger for Fifer, the kindest friend to all Beckfordian children, simply because he is Chapelviller, simply because he is Christian."

David knew he had his audience. He could see it in each and every eye. The eyes said, "this is not fair. We will do what we can to save Fifer."

David continued, "well, we are Beckfordian children. We are called the precious jewels of Beckfordian union. We are loved and cared for like no other children in the world and then we are asked to master our education. But we will not master any education today, we will not master any instructions today. Instead we will march to Sinclair Circle to see the Esau and we will tell the Esau that we will not return to school until Fifer is free."

David could see the doubt on most of their faces. He knew he dared not let the doubt linger.

One little boy raised his hand and asked, "why not just call the Esau on the phone?"

David answered quickly, he had anticipated the question. “Because we cannot speak as one on a phone. Only a united, strong, display will convince the adults, the adults of understanding.”

David saw that his classmates understood.

“My plan,” he said, “will not fail, cannot fail, there will be no disgrace in trying, there will be no scandal, only respect will be attached to our names. We, the united fourth graders. Education is too important to the adults for us to fail.” David saw that everyone agreed with him. The lingering doubt was gone. “Besides,” he added, “there is a touch of mischief in this. Think, fourth graders, little picknys standing up to adults.”

That did it. That totally convinced them. For children are children the world over, and what child can resist a mischief?

-5-

The children were on their way, walking with purpose on the narrow country road that led to Sinclair Circle. School had been cancelled for the day under the authority of the headmaster, Mr. Cullen.

Dora, enjoying the mischief more so than anyone else, had insisted that she be the one to go and tell the headmaster.

Mr. Cullen, a tall, thin, light-skinned, elderly man, had been at a loss. His only choice, as he saw it, was to cancel school for the day and to hurriedly call to notify the parents.

Oh, the parents will be at school alright, thought David, coming fast on the run as if the Christian devil was chasing them. But we, the fourth graders, are not going to be there. We are going to be on the road. On the road to Sinclair Circle. To see old man Esau.

The Esau had a lot of influence in Beckford. It is said that the Esau could feel genetic outcomes. So it was his responsibility to approve adults for marriage. If the Esau felt that a resulting offspring would be bad for Beckford, the marriage would not take place. The Esau therefore held a lot of influence in Beckford but he did not have the most influence. That distinction belonged to the Council of Women Elders.

David knew that the Council would meet him somewhere along the road and that he would have to beat the Council in order to get to the Esau. Okay, thought little David, I know that I am ready.

-6-

Sure enough the parents were coming alright. Those who had rushed to the school in their cars had to park their cars and leave them behind because the fourth graders spread out across the narrow road and steadfastly ignored the bleating of the car horns. So the parents abandoned their cars but they would not, could not, abandon their children, as their picknys trekked on this strange strange journey, insistently walking the whole two miles to Sinclair Circle.

What was a parent to do? First came that strange phone call explaining that their little fourth graders were not going to be in school. Now look at them, marching away like little soldiers.

It did not help when a parent walked up to a little fourth grader and asked him or her to return to school. Beckfordian children are raised, drilled, indoctrinated to be polite so there was no disrespect in their voices as they answered, “I’m sorry mom, I’m sorry dad, but we are going to save Fifer. I cannot return with you.”

But the worst part, the very worst part was that there was a hint of mischief in those ever so polite answers. What was a parent to do? Nothing. They could do nothing, so they, like zombies, dutifully followed behind.

-7-

They were a half-mile into their journey, steadfastly ignoring their parents, secure in the knowledge that Beckfordian parents did not spank or bully their children. It was Dora who suggested that the boys and girls sing the different roles in the childhood song of “Children, Children.” There were shouts of agreement. The girls started first.

“Children, Children.”

“Yes, Ma-maah.”

“Where have you been to?”

“Grandma-maah.”

“What she gave you?”

“Bun and cheese.”

“Where is my share?”

“Up in the air.”

“How can I reach it?”

“Climb on a broken chair.”

“Suppose I fall.”

“We don’t care!”

“Who taught you those manners?”

“The dog.”

“Who’s the dog?”

“You!”

The children broke up into laughter. This was so much fun! It was now the boys turn to start the song. They never got the chance.

Ahead, blocking their path was Mother Mary of the Council of Women Elders and with her was the Beckfordian Legend herself, Mrs. Dorothy Sinclair.

Mother Mary of course was elderly. She leaned upon her walking stick. She was a dark-skinned woman with friendly eyes. Friendly eyes or not, the children were afraid of her wisdom. Every child knew that one did not get to be leader of the Council unless one was very wise. It was not her wisdom though that caused David to be afraid. It was the Beckfordian

Legend, Mrs. Dorothy Sinclair. Everyone knew that Mrs. Sinclair was the best at using psychology. David had not anticipated her being here.

The children came closer but not too close. That would have been disrespectful.

Mother Mary addressed David directly.

"David Stoner, I was informed by headmaster Cullen that you are the ringleader of this…of this rebellion. I cannot, respectfully, out of my duty to Beckford, allow you to go any further."

David was not afraid. He knew in his heart that it was not Mother Mary who was the stumbling block here. With a defiant force of will he restrained himself from looking at Mrs. Sinclair.

"We must save Fifer," was all he said.

Mother Mary thought for a short while. "Okay, child, okay, I'll make a deal with you, a Challenge of Wisdom, if you beat Mrs. Sinclair and myself, you can go to see the Esau with all my blessings. If you fail, you will return to school."

David had to agree. If he refused the challenge he knew his classmates would no longer follow him. The respect in which all children held the Council would be too much to overcome even for the life of Fifer.

As he was thinking Mother Mary said, "okay young David, let us begin. The first challenge is Mrs. Sinclair. If you win then I will challenge you."

David could say nothing. He only nodded. It was impolite to nod one's head to an adult, especially to the elderly, but Mother Mary seemed not to notice.

David finally looked at Mrs. Sinclair. He wished he did not have to. Even though a pickny, he knew. She was so beautiful. Black skin, eyes almost Chinese in their almond-like shape, nose flared on her mature beautiful face. Why did she have to be here? She was best at using psychology, every Beckfordian knew that.

Mrs. Sinclair spoke, her voice friendly, "young David," she said, "I have only one question for you, by what right do you seek to deny our Beckfordian children their education?"

David was stumped. He indeed had no right, no right at all. He had lost. Fifer would die because he was not wise enough.

Think David. Think, he commanded his brain. The answer lies somewhere.

David was partially right. The answer did lie somewhere, but it did not lie in his brain. The answer laid in little Dora's brain. It laid there because she prided herself on knowing everything about her idol, Mrs. Dorothy Sinclair, the Beckfordian Legend.

Dora came forward and stood beside David. She was shaking with nervousness to be so close to her idol. Still, she did not let nervousness stop her. Dora leaned towards David's ear. "Asked her how it felt to use Christian words to win the Formal Speech Contest." David understood. He asked the question.

Mrs. Dorothy Sinclair was stunned. She knew she had lost. She bowed not to David but to Dora, the little fourth grader who had somehow bested her. Dora bowed in return. She was no longer so nervous.

"It felt," said Mrs. Sinclair, "it felt dirty, as if someone had thrown a large bucket of refuse all over me.

"Yes," answered David, "we know," he turned his head and shoulders, extending his arm, indicating all of the fourth graders, "if we do not save Fifer, we will feel dirty all our lives. No amount of Beckfordian education will ever prevent that. We shall be damaged all our lives. Beckfordians do not damage their children. In our history we have been damaged enough. For we were once slaves in South Carolina."

"Yes, child," said Dorothy, conceding the victory, "we have been damaged enough."

Dorothy turned her head to look at Mother Mary. A little smile played in the corner of her lips. Funny, thought David, her expression does not look like one of defeat at all.

He did not have time to think about it. Mother Mary was ready with her challenge.

"Young David," she said, "how can any Beckfordian, even a child, place Beckford at risk by asking us to involve ourselves in Jamaican Law?"

David was ready. He had anticipated such a question.

"Ma'am," he answered, "Beckford is always at risk. So, at risk, that we have created two other circles to protect us. Beckford is called the First Circle. The Third Circle is our spies that work overseas. The Second

Circle…no one knows where the Second Circle is located. They protect us in case our old enemy, the Hand, should attack us. They protect us though we know not where they are. It is so because Beckford is always at risk. So risk is not the problem. So I wonder ma'am, do we refuse to help Fifer because he is Chapelviller? Because he is Christian? Because we are prejudiced?"

Everyone, almost in union, gasped.

Beckfordian prejudice, against Christianity, was something hardly anyone ever talked about. And here was this young boy broadcasting their shame. Even to the fourth graders, the shame stung. It was as if scandal had plunged its sharpened talons into their little hearts. It was shameful for them but not as shameful as it was for Mother Mary.

There were actual tears in her revered old eyes. She wiped away the tears.

She regained her dignity and her voice.

"Young David, you have won your challenge. This day belongs to you. Go to the Esau." She hobbled aside. The fourth graders started to move forward.

"But," said Mother Mary, "though the day is yours, tomorrow will belong to the Council." The children stopped, sensing that she had something wise to say. "In all my time on the Council young David, I have searched for one Beckfordian to become an expert on the Christian Bible. It seemed to me to be important. But not one Beckfordian would even consider the notion. It seemed my search would end in futility. Perhaps not so now. I now know where to look."

She stared into the very heart of young David's eyes.

-8-

The Esau was waiting for them. He stood before his little green house on the edge of a picturesque orange grove. He was old, older even than Mother Mary. He leaned his small brown body against his walking stick.

He smiled at them. There were no longer any teeth in his mouth. The sparkle in his eyes told the children that they were welcome.

"I know why you are here," the Esau announced. The words rumbled out of his toothless old mouth. "Mother Mary called me. She told me some interesting things about you children, and I have been thinking about your problem. But before I say more…the oranges are ripe in my grove and I, well, Patrick, my assistant, have prepared some of the oranges, juicy and sweet, for all of you." He raised his eyes to include the trailing parents.

A tall young man emerged from the little house carrying a large white basin pan filled with peeled oranges. The children almost bolted for the oranges but some sense of decorum still developing in their little fourth grade brains held them back. Patrick passed among them, smiling, as the children gorged themselves. The adults watched, confused. Patrick offered the remaining oranges to the adults. They accepted of course, least they showed any disrespect to the Esau. But the parents only picked distractedly at their treat.

The Esau cleared his old throat. It did not sound like much of a clearing. But the fourth graders understood that it was now time for the Esau's answer. The children stood at attention; perfect little soldiers who had gone on a long crusade to save the life of Fifer. Deep down, they already knew what the Esau would say. But they could not leave, would not even think of leaving, until the Esau spoke the words.

The Esau spoke: "Children, young David, young Marcia, young Dora, I have been told that you are the organizers of this…of this procession. Well done, well done to all of you fourth graders. I, Esau Sinclair, I give you my word that I will free Fifer."

The shouting roar was tremendous. The children jumped and danced and hugged each other with great joy. The Esau's promise to them was written in stone. Though they had no idea where the expression "written in stone" came from.

Finally, the children settled down.

The Esau spoke again, "it will take me some time to free Fifer, perhaps two or three months. But Fifer will be free. Now return to school, tomorrow. And let not one of you be late."

The idea of being late had never entered any of their little fourth grade minds.

-9-

David, Marcia and Dora walked ahead of the other children. The other children were too busy playing. As is universal, the world over, the boys were picking on the girls and the girls were protesting, a little too loudly, that they did not like the attention.

Marcia did not like the attention that Dora was paying to David. Dora was acting as if she did not know that David was her pickny friend. She had better find another pickny friend to pay attention to. But Marcia was not going to do anything about it, not going to do anything about it - today.

"David?" Marcia said, "I'm glad we saved Fifer, or will save him. David nodded. "But I don't understand why he was so important to you. None of us thought to save him. Why was he so important to you?"

Marcia could tell that nosy Dora was listening. She didn't care. She wanted David's answer.

David was thinking. "I suppose it has to do with Santa Claus," he said. He saw the immediate confusion in their eyes. He moved to take away the confusion. "There is not a Santa Claus in Beckford. Santa is a Christian tradition. We cannot have a Santa in Beckford. The closest we ever had was Fifer." Both girls nodded.

David continued, "I heard something on the radio a few months ago. A young man was talking. He said that Santa did not bring presents to poor children and that was proof for him, when he was a poor small child, that Santa was not real. And then he said that just as there is no Santa Claus that lives at the North Pole, likewise there is no Christ that lives in Heaven. At first, I agreed with the young man. I am Beckfordian after all." His two companions nodded in agreement. They too are Beckfordians after all.

"But," said David, a few days later Fifer brought me a *brand new* fife. I had lost mine in the Beckford river. I had not yet requested a new one. But there was Fifer with a new one, just for me. I was so happy and somehow, I just knew that the young man on the radio was in some ways wrong. Christ may not live in Heaven, but I just knew, I just knew where Christ does live. I knew." He said no more.

"Where?" said both girls. In union, speaking in one voice, they said, "Where does Christ live?"

"Christ," said David, "Christ lives in the hearts and minds of people like Fifer."

-The End-
(for now)

<u>The Lesson - A Humanic Fable</u>

by Indy Jean Arden

-1-

Jon Christian was ten years old and he did not want to go to America. He was going to have to go though because his father, Paul Christian, was in America teaching psychology at some university. Jon was not even sure what psychology was. He was sure though that it was some kind of adult stuff - not for children, not for picknys.

Jon smiled, he liked the new word pickny. No one called you a pickny in Saint Samaritan. It was only in Jamaica that the term was used for a child. John had laughed because he liked the sound of the new word, "pickny," and he liked the mature way in which the ten-year-old girl had spoken. So he had decided to be her friend, and that was how he discovered that the island of Saint Samaritan was a special place to live.

-2-

What he discovered was something he knew all along because of course his mom and dad had told him. He had paid little attention. He had of course learned his country's history in first grade and second grade and third grade; he had paid little attention, except when he had to recall it for a test. He had received the best grade, and then forgot that his island nation was indeed special, made up of special people; made up of Christian people. It was through the visiting Jamaicans when he followed his new friend to a celebration that he learned to appreciate his country.

They were all sitting around in the large dining room of the hotel and the Jamaicans were talking in their funny accents. Jon understood them though. He sat next to his new friend. Her name was Maria. She was dark in complexion, while he was brown. Jon thought she was very beautiful but he could never tell her that because children did not tell other children that they were beautiful. Every boy knew that. They had to wait till they were teenagers or something. By that time Maria would be back in Jamaica and Jon would not have to tell her at all. Jon breathed a sigh of relief.

Someone was speaking. “It was in the year of nineteen forty-nine that the great storm did hit Saint Samaritan. Many lives were lost. Saint Samaritan was basically ruined. Then came the Americans, with their great planes and their great ships; then came their soldiers, with their physical strength and their generosity of spirit and their big voices and their big smiles. And they rebuilt Saint Samaritan. Rebuilt it so well that now Saint Samaritan is called the Jewel of the Caribbean; and we come here every year to celebrate and give thanks and aye even to raise a glass or two in appreciation of America. For every Samaritan knows that indeed Americans are indeed a gracious people.”

Everyone, except for Jon, shouted “Aye, aye, aye, America, America, America!”

-3-

Jon felt funny. He had never appreciated America. The country that rebuilt his country, made his country rich with tourist dollars. Jon felt funny. He had never said a prayer to Christ in appreciation of America. Jon rose up. He was going to church to give thanks for the Americans. He had completely forgotten about Maria. He was not even aware that Maria was following him.

"Where are you going?" she asked.

Jon stopped. "Oh, I'm sorry. I forgot you were with me but I must go to church to pray."

"Why?" she asked.

"I must go and give thanks to America," he answered.

Maria did not understand. Her face knotted in confusion. "America has everything," she said, "no one needs to pray for them."

"No, no, I am not going to pray for them. I am going to church, to give thanks to them for rebuilding my country, for rebuilding Saint Samaritan."

Maria was still confused. "I do not think you should go to church," she said, "church can be very dangerous."

"No, it cannot," responded Jon, "church is the safest place in the world."

"No, it is not," responded Maria, "church is where you learn the slave plantation mindset."

Now it was Jon's turn to be confused.

-4-

"What is the slave plantation mindset?" asked Jon.

Maria hesitated. She did not want to answer, but she did answer.

"It...it is how you think, in your mind, that blacks are supposed to be second class."

Jon had never heard of such a thing. Indeed he had never really thought of what it meant to be black or white or to be any color...except when he was at school and he was taught that his fore parents had been slaves on the sugar cane plantations of Saint Samaritan. He had never liked learning about that. It was a very uncomfortable feeling. But then would come recess and he would forget all about slavery.

"But we are not second class anymore," said Jon. "We are rich, and everyone comes here to enjoy themselves. We are respected."

"Yes," said Maria, "Saint Samaritan is rich but the rest of the Caribbean is poor. I learned that in school. To be poor and black and Christian is to have the slave plantation mindset. I learned that in my home."

"Your home?"

"Yes, my hometown of Beckford, Jamaica."

"Is Beckford poor?"

Maria laughed. "No, no, Beckford is the richest place in the world for we do not care about money and we do not build any churches which cost money." Maria resumed her laughter.

"You confuse me," said Jon, "How can Beckford be the richest place in the world? Jamaica is a poor country."

Maria thought for a few moments. "My mom told me that we are mainly rich because of the smart people that we produce. We send them to foreign, overseas, to study science and business and psychology and adult stuff like that, and then we open banks all over the world, banks that we Beckfordians can get money from. My mom says that we have been doing it for a long time and that we are quite ex…expert at it, so that we are all rich."

"Oh, I see," said Jon, "you own banks."

"Yes, we do," Maria said proudly. "Beckfordians are not regular Jamaicans, though regular Jamaicans are nice people too, even though they go to church."

Jon was losing interest in Maria. He did not care if her people - The Beckfordians - were rich. He had a prayer to get to.

He started walking away from her.

"Wait," she said, "you can't go without me."

Of course, he could. She was not from Saint Samaritan. She was only a visitor, a tourist. But…but there was something about her face. A pleading…and he could not leave her there with that look upon her face. It would not be the gentlemanly thing to do. It would be mean. His dad had always taught him to look out for girls, to be a gentleman. He did not want to let down his dad, though he had taken off and gone to America and soon he too and his mom was going to have to go and join him there. Perhaps though in America they did not have pretty dark-skinned girls with pleading eyes like that.

"Okay," he said softly, "you can come with me."

She hesitated. "Not before I tell my mom and dad and get their permission. Will you wait for me?"

He nodded.

She turned around and took off running.

Jon was surprised at how fast she ran. Then he remembered his parents watching the Caribbean Games and commenting about how fast the Jamaican runners were. "They dominate the sprint races," his mom had said. Then she started bragging about how fast she was when she was a girl. Dad had started laughing, then stopped when mom looked at him sternly. But Jon had agreed with his dad for every boy knew that a mother could never have been a fast runner. But Maria had been so fast... perhaps mom had been fast... naah, mom was just bragging.

Maria returned, skipping and nodding her head, smiling.

"Mom and dad gave me permission. I must return before dusk. Will it take you long to pray?"

"No, prayers are usually short, especially for children, for children do not have much to say - unlike adults."

The children laughed. Jon started skipping towards the church for no good reason except that it was fun and Maria skipped alongside him.

-5-

"We are being followed," said Maria.

Jon stopped walking and turned around.

Maria laughed. "You would not be able to see him or her. Some adult Beckfordians are trained not to be seen if they do not want to be. My parents sent him or her to make sure that I am safe. That was the only way they would allow me to come with you. Beckfordians are very protective of their children."

"All parents are very protective of their children," Jon was very sure. "And Saint Samaritan is very safe, there is very little crime here, it says so on the news."

"My parents are Beckfordians, they would have to make sure. It's just the way they are," said Maria.

"They love you, they protect you."

Maria nodded.

Jon was thinking. "Your parents are like Christ. Christ protects us. Those of us who believe in him. He protects us."

"I do not know any religion," said Maria. "There are no churches in Beckford. That is why I'm coming with you. I have never been into a church. Beckfordians are afraid of churches."

Jon stopped walking and held her hands. He looked into her eyes. "There is nothing to be afraid of. It is just a building - a church - where you kneel and talk to God - to Christ. You just talk to Him."

"I know," answered Maria, "It is not the building or the praying that I'm afraid of. That part is okay."

"Then what are you afraid of?"

Maria did not know how to answer.

They resumed walking.

"I'm afraid that if I go to church it will teach me to think of blacks as second class. All Beckfordians are afraid of that, that is why there are no churches in Beckford." Maria hanged her head as if she was ashamed to speak anymore.

"Oh, I see," said Jon. But he really did not see. I am only ten years old, he thought. This is adult stuff. I do not know how to help Maria. But…but all his life he had been taught to help girls. And now he could not. He felt ashamed. He just knew, he just knew that if he was an adult he would know how to help her. It sucks being a child. Children knew nothing. He wished his father was here but he had to go, he had to go all the way to America. There was no father to turn to. He was going to help Maria all by himself.

-6-

"When we go into the church to pray I won't say anything that will make you feel bad about being black," Jon promised.

"I know that Jon," responded Maria, "you are a gentleman, you are kind and thoughtful. You did not leave me to go to your prayer. You are taking me to see you talk to your God. I want to see you do it. If I feel bad about it, I will tell you."

"Okay, it is a deal," he said.

-7-

They walked slowly down the center of the church, holding hands. They did not speak. Jon noticed that Maria kept turning her head. She had never been in a church before. How could he help her to know it was truly okay? There was no harm here. But she already knew that. It was a different kind of harm. The kind of harm that affected adults - black adults. He is not an adult, so it was the kind of harm that he would not know about. He wanted to know though. He wanted to know so that he could help her. Perhaps if he prayed. Isn't that what God is for?

Jon kneeled in front of the cross. He could sense Maria's eyes, staring into his back. It did not matter of course; she is only curious.

"Lord Jesus," he played. "I came here because I feel that I should. I did not want to wait till Sunday. I am ten years old and all my life I have heard the story of how the great storm had almost destroyed Saint Samaritan and how the Americans came and rebuilt our country and it never occurred to me to give thanks to the Americans. I know that my people are grateful for the Americans but I never gave thanks to them or to you. Was it not you who sent them? Was it not you that rebuilt Saint Samaritan? If I do not thank the Americans, am I then not thanking you?

"In the name of Jesus, I thank the Americans, I thank you Lord.

"My parents taught me to be proud. Would I be proud if we were a poor people? We are a rich people because the Americans made us a tourist destination. Everyone comes here. They bring their money and we give them joy. My mom says that we got the better of the deal. I do not know, I am only a child.

"And finally, Lord, will you help Maria? I do not want her to be afraid of church. Perhaps you, dear God, could build a church in Beckford. Perhaps then she would see, perhaps then she would understand. Thank you, Lord. Amen"

-8-

They were returning back to the hotel, holding hands.

"I'm glad you included me in your prayers Jon. It made me feel special, like you cared about me - like I was your girlfriend." Maria laughed. Jon did not see any humor in the situation.

"We are too young to be boyfriend and girlfriend," Jon declared, "maybe if we were teenagers."

"Yeah, I know," Maria giggled. "I can't believe I'll be a teenager someday. I like being a pickny."

They walked, swinging hands.

"Jon."

"Yes."

"I think the problem was slavery. I think that is what my people are afraid of. I think they are afraid that slavery will come back. Beckfordians, we think slavery and church are one and the same."

Jon did not say anything for a while.

"No," said Jon, "slavery will not come back, the Americans will not allow it. They saved us, they made us rich. They are powerful and they are decent. My father would never live in a country that was not decent."

"I believe you Jon. I do not understand why my people are afraid. But I did like hearing you pray. It seemed harmless. When I'm a teenager I'll take a Beckfordian boy to church - somewhere, if not in Beckford."

-9-

"Jon."

"Yes."

"Is there a place we can sit? There is something I must tell you about a lesson that I learned today."

Jon thought for a while. "Perhaps up ahead. I think I can make a comfortable spot for us."

He led her to the edge of the banana grove.

"Here? I do not see a comfortable spot."

"Aaah," he said, "but I am a resourceful Samaritan boy. See those dried banana leaves hanging from that bunch of banana trees?"

"Yes."

"Watch," he instructed.

He pulled on the dry leaf with his left hand and with a swift upward punch of his right hand he freed the dry leaf from the banana tree. He did this several times. Then he collected the leaves and rolled them into two tight circles.

"My lady," he said, "a comfortable seat for both of us."

Maria almost laughed with delight, instead she just beamed at him, silent laughter registering in the smile of her lips. And so, they sat, comfortable, enjoying a respite from the tropical afternoon sun, in the shade of the banana grove.

"Quite a resourceful boy," was all she said.

He beamed too, but not with a look of silent laughter. He beamed with a look of boyish pride.

-10-

"I learned a lesson today," said Maria. She said no more.

Jon waited. And would have waited for a thousand years if that was how long it would have taken. For he knew she would speak again. Still…still he was glad it only took a few moments.

"My mother is always trying to teach me new things," said Maria. "And I must tell you that sometimes I do not always want to listen." Maria lowered her voice, "because at ten-years-old, of course, I already know everything."

They both laughed, howled. It was the funniest thing in the world because they both knew that at ten they knew so very little.

The laughter went away and neither one of them could tell just where the laughter went. Still…still it was good to know that laughter lurked somewhere, somewhere very close, always at the ready to once again refresh the soul.

"One of the things my mother helped me with is developing my vocabulary. She is big on that. She says 'you are a Beckfordian young lady and a Beckfordian young lady must, must always speak well.' So, I try.

"One of the most recent vocabulary words is graciousness. I thought I knew the definition. I thought it was thoughtfulness and a kind demeanor. I was wrong. Today I saw -"

"That is what it means," interrupted Jon.

"Yes, you are right. But you are also wrong. I saw the meaning today. I saw the meaning in you. That is the lesson I learned."

It does not require maturity to clean out your ears with stillness and a closed mouth and lend such a clean ear to the voice of discovery.

"When I saw you praying, when I heard you praying, you prayed not for yourself or even for your family. You simply gave thanks for the brave and gracious Americans. You even somewhat chastised yourself for not giving thanks earlier. I was struck by your words. I was struck by your graciousness and suddenly I knew a new definition of the word. A definition I would never have found even in gracious Beckford. The definition of graciousness is oneness. We are all God's children. All of us are one in His sight. That we separate - segregate - ourselves that is the devil's work. And I can prove it.

-11-

Again, Jon's clean ears yearned only to listen.

"When the Americans came to rebuild Saint Samaritan, they showed their graciousness. They are a kind and thoughtful people. Today, in church, on your knees, you showed your thoughtfulness, you showed your kindness; you showed your oneness with the Americans. Though their graciousness took place a long time ago, today, you showed your oneness with them."

-12-

Jon knew that Maria had proven her point. There was no way he could argue with her. Funny, all he wanted to do was give thanks to the Americans and to God, and he ended up teaching a lesson like he was an adult or something. No way! It was more fun being a child.

"There is only one more thing I want to say Jon," resumed Maria. "When I return to Beckford, I will not ask the elders to build a church. I know that they will refuse me. I will ask them to build a house of grace, but I think I can get them to design it to look like a church. Beckfordians are very protective of their children, as I told you earlier, and they are also very indulgent to their picknys. I think I can get a church to come to Beckford, if I am most gracious in my request."

The children laughed. Laughter had been sitting on their shoulders all along. Oh! What fun it was to trick adults!

-The End-
(for now)

Note: Jon Christian will return in "The School Yard," a much darker fable.

About the Author

Born in 1984 to a Jamaican mother and a British father, Indy Jean Arden never felt at home anywhere. Not in Jamaica, where she attended grammar school, not in England, or Connecticut, USA, where she attended high school. She started writing as a means of coping. In college she noticed that almost everything she wrote was somewhat controversial, involving religious and social issues. She continued on that path. It was her way of not stilling her voice.

Now divorced, she teaches in a small conservative Jamaican town where no one (except for her two young children) know that she writes. She wants to keep it that way and uses proxies to facilitate getting her works published.

www.ingramcontent.com/pod-product-compliance
Lightning Source LLC
LaVergne TN
LVHW080557160826
845677LV00010B/1888

* 9 7 9 8 3 7 4 6 3 0 5 9 6 *